WAFFLE THE POP DOG

Published in the UK by Scholastic Children's Books, 2020
Euston House, 24 Eversholt Street, London, NW1 1DB
A division of Scholastic Limited

London ~ New York ~ Toronto ~ Sydney ~ Auckland
Mexico City ~ New Delhi ~ Hong Kong

SCHOLASTIC and associated logos are trademarks and/or
registered trademarks of Scholastic Inc.

Waffle The Wonder Dog © and TM Darrall Macqueen Ltd 2020
Written by Emily Stead © Scholastic Children's Books
Cover background image created by Freepik

DARRALL MACQUEEN LTD

TRADE EDITION ISBN 978 07023 0079 0
SCHOLASTIC CLUBS AND FAIRS EDITION ISBN 978 07023 0074 5

A CIP catalogue record for this book is available from the British Library.

Printed in China
Papers used by Scholastic Children's Books are made from wood grown in sustainable forests.

2 4 6 8 10 9 7 5 3 1

www.scholastic.co.uk

When Doug decided he wanted to be in the school show, he asked Waffle to help him. Doug was trying a trick called ventriloquism, where he pretended to speak in Waffle's voice. Waffle had to open and close his mouth, but he wasn't allowed to talk. But things weren't quite going to plan...

"My name is Waffle!" Doug began, trying not to move his mouth.

"No, it isn't!" Waffle replied.

"Waffle! I said don't talk!" laughed Doug. "Let's try again."

"Okay!" Waffle woofed again.

"Waffle!" groaned Doug.

Just then, Simon came in from the garden. "What are you two doing?" he asked.

"I've been trying out ventriloquism for the school show," Doug explained. "But Waffle keeps talking!"

"Hmm," said Simon. "Why not do something you're already good at?"

While Doug tried to think of something
else to do, Waffle did something he was
really good at ... licking plates clean!
   "Oh no you don't, Waffle!" smiled Simon,
closing the dishwasher door.

In the kitchen, Simon picked up a wooden spoon and
began tapping out a tune on the kitchen pots and pans.
"How about music?" said Simon. "Waf-fle dog-gy!" he sang.
Doug decided to try it. "You're such a cle-ver dog, such a
cle-ver dog, you are!" he sang, tapping in time.

6

Then, Waffle had a good idea. "Do music at the show!" he barked.

"That's brilliant!" smiled Doug, and he hurried upstairs to his bedroom to get started.

A little while later, Doug was ready to show Simon and Waffle his musical inventions.

"Wow! Look at these instruments you've made," gasped Simon. "Well done, Doug!"

There were shakers, horns and a drum kit made from recycled bits and bobs. Simon and Doug decided to test them out. *BANG! BANG! CRASH!* went Simon on the drums. And, *TAP! TAP! TAP!* went Doug. Waffle joined in on the bells. *TINKLE! TINKLE!*

Suddenly, there was another *BASH-BASH-BASH*-ing sound. It was Mrs Hobbs from next door, banging on the wall. "Keep the noise down!" she shouted.

"Sorry, Mrs Hobbs," Simon called back. "We just can't stop!"

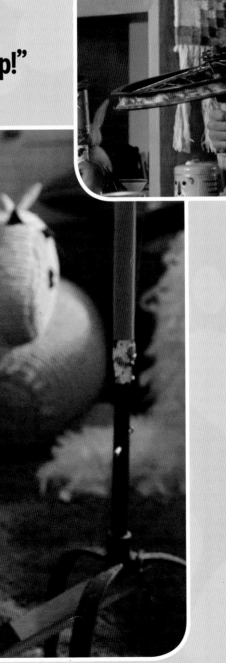

Just then, Doug told everyone to stop playing.
"Listen!" he said. "Mrs Hobbs is banging on the wall in time to our beat ...
and she's really good!"
She was so good that Doug decided to invite Mrs Hobbs to join the band!

"You call those instruments?" said Mrs Hobbs
grumpily after seeing Doug's inventions. "They need
to go straight in the recycling box!"

But Doug wasn't giving up. "Please, Mrs Hobbs," he begged. "You'd be great on the drums!"

"Well, I'm sure I could do better than Waffle," she agreed.

So, Mrs Hobbs sat down at the drum kit and began bashing out a mega beat! Doug and Simon were amazed!

Simon joined in with Mrs Hobbs. *BASH! BASH! BASH! BOP! BOP! BOP!*
"Wait!" shouted Doug. "What should I do for the school show?"
Simon knew. "You need a song!" he said.

So Doug, Simon and Mrs Hobbs came up with a song together. Doug began to sing, but he couldn't think of a last line that rhymed, until helpful Waffle lent a paw.
"It's fun to have family,
And it's fun to have friends,
The fun we have..."
"It never ends!" added Waffle.

Doug began dancing and he was still moving when the music stopped. This time, it was Mrs Hobbs and Simon's turn to be impressed by Doug's amazing moves. They clapped their hands while Waffle barked three cheers. "Woof! Woof! Woof!"

"I can dance, too" smiled Doug. "Now I can sing *and* dance for the school show!"

"You will, Doug!" said Simon proudly.
"And all your family and friends will be there to watch."
Doug and Simon shared a big hug.
"Woof!" barked Waffle, wagging his tail.

When Evie and Jess arrived home, the house was very quiet. "Waffle? Doug?" called Evie.

"Where is everyone?" wondered Jess.

They went upstairs and were surprised to find Simon setting up some lights and Mrs Hobbs sitting at a drum kit.

"Welcome to the Brooklyn-Bell-Hobbs' first performance," Mrs Hobbs announced grandly. "Featuring Waffle the Dog!"

Simon showed Evie and Jess to their seats, ready for the show.
"Put your hands together for the talent behind it all ...
it's Doug!" Mrs Hobbs exclaimed.

Evie and Jess clapped and cheered excitedly. They couldn't wait for the show to get started!

"Let's do this!" smiled Doug.

"Woof!" barked Waffle.

Mrs Hobbs counted them in ...

"One, two, one, two, three!"

Doug showed off his best dance moves as the Brooklyn-Bell-Hobbs band all sang and played their instruments together. It was so much fun that Evie and Jess joined in too!

Soon, the Brooklyn-Bell family were all singing together, "It's fun to have family, And it's fun to have friends, The fun we have, it never ends!"

As the song came to an end, Simon blew loudly on Doug's homemade trombeloona. It made a very funny sound: "*Brr-rrr-rumph!*"

"That was fantastic!" said Jess, giving Doug a big hug.

"Amazing dancing, Doug!" added Evie.

"Music! Love music!" woofed Waffle.

And everybody laughed.

Click!

"Come on, everybody," said Jess. "Selfie time!"
Everybody smiled as Jess took a photo on her
phone — they would always remember the first ever
performance by the Brooklyn-Bell-Hobbs band.
Now, thanks to Waffle's wonderful idea, Doug was
ready for his school show.